MERRY CHRISTMAS 2007
FROM GXPOCE

D0517227

The Night the Lights Went Out on S

Written by Steve Van Bakel
Illustrated by Anna Palfrey

Tall Tales Press Book Publishing Inc.

Text Copyright © 2003 Steve Van Bakel
Illustrations Copyright © 2003 Anna Palfrey
Printed and Bound in Canada

All rights reserved. No part of this publication may be reproduced, stored in a retrieval system or transmitted, in any form or by any means, without the prior express written permission of Tall Tales Press Book Publishing Inc. or, in the case of photocopying or other reprographic copying, a license from CANCOPY (Canadian Copyright Licensing Agency), 1 Young St., Suite 1900, Toronto, ON M5E 1E5, FAX (416) 868-1621.

Published by
Tall Tales Press Book Publishing Inc.
20 Tuscany Valley Park NW
Calgary, AB
T3L 2B6

National Library of Canada Cataloguing in Publication Data
Van Bakel, Steve, 1966-
The night the lights went out on Santa / written by Steve Van Bakel ;
illustrated by Anna Palfrey.

ISBN 0-9733087-0-2

1. Santa Claus—Juvenile fiction. I. Palfrey, Anna, 1969- II. Title.

PS8593.A53825N53 2003 jC813'.6 C2003-911133-4

For My Daughter Grace and My Wife Rayn.
- Steve Van Bakel
For Roger, Spencer and Graham
-Anna Palfrey

The Night the Lights Went Out on Santa

Written by Steve Van Bakel
Illustrated by Anna Palfrey

Tall Tales Press Book Publishing Inc.

With milk and cookies lovingly placed near the tree for Santa, Grace's mom announced that it was time for bed.

"But Mommy," Grace said, "we have to leave something for the reindeer!"

"Quick like a bunny then, it is far past your bedtime," her mother said.

Hopping like a bunny, Grace went to the fridge and found a handful of carrots that she placed next to Santa's milk and cookies. After double checking that her note to Santa was still under the glass of milk, Grace was finally ready for bed.

"**M**ommy, do you think Santa and his reindeer will be okay in the storm?" Grace asked, as her mother tucked the young girl into bed.

"It's pretty bad out there tonight," her mother replied. "I think we had better say an extra prayer that Santa has a safe night."

"That's a great idea," Grace said excitedly, as she started into her prayers. She finished with, "And please watch over Santa and his reindeer tonight so that they have a safe night and are able to visit children all over the world."

"Goodnight, Sweety," Grace's mother said as she kissed her daughter.

"Is the nightlight on?" Grace asked.

"Check," her mother replied.

"My flashlight is still beside the bed?"

"Check," her mother said, as she reached down and flicked on the flashlight to prove that it was there and in working order.

"And you will leave the door open a bit, right?" Grace asked concerned.

"Just like always," her mother promised. "Now have a good night. I love you."

"I love you too, Mommy."

As Grace's mother left the room, she made sure that the door was left open just enough to allow a little light to enter the room from the hallway. This was a nightly routine for Grace and her mother; you see Grace was afraid of the dark.

Grace wasn't sure how long she had been asleep, but she suddenly awoke feeling strange. She tried to open her eyes, but that didn't work, it was still dark in her room. She tried again and this time she realized that her eyes were open but all the lights in the house were out. At first she was afraid, but then she remembered the flashlight beside her bed.

CLICK! The flashlight came on and the room was flooded with light.

Not wanting to risk losing her only light, Grace went around her room and found each of her battery powered lights. Every Christmas Grace had asked Santa to bring her a new light to help fight her fear of the dark. Santa was very resourceful and each year he left a different kind of light tucked in her Christmas stocking. Last year it was a battery-powered camping lantern, the year before that it was a flashlight that you could wear on your head like a miner's lamp.

As she found each light, she turned it on to make her room even brighter.

Right about the same time Grace woke to a darkened bedroom, somebody not too far away was also encountering problems.

It was Christmas eve and Santa was used to running into storms as he delivered toys to children all over the world. In fact, he often welcomed the refreshing snowflakes that helped keep him and his reindeer cool as they flew across the night sky.

But this year, the storm was different. Instead of bringing the cooling soft snowflakes to soothe his reindeer, the storm brought driving, heavy ice. The ice was building up on the reindeer and the sled and the extra weight was making flying very difficult.

"Hang in there guys," Santa hollered to the reindeer. He wasn't sure if they could still hear him over the ice storm, but he continued to shout words of encouragement.

"Keep up the good work. It's not far now."

"Wait. There it is!" Santa called out. "Just ahead, I see the lights of our next town."

And just in time Santa thought; his reindeer were exhausted and they needed to rest, and allow some of the ice to melt from their bodies and antlers.

Just as Santa sighed with relief, all the lights in the town, including the Christmas lights, suddenly disappeared.

Peeking from her bedroom window, Grace saw that the lights had gone out in the entire town. It was still blowing ice and snow and she could see that icicles were building up on the hydro lines and light poles. It must be the storm that knocked all the power out, Grace thought.

But she had an idea!

With a flashlight in one hand, a camp lantern in the other, and with her head lamp on, Grace decided to sneak downstairs to see if Santa had been to her house yet. If he had, Grace knew that she would find a new flashlight somewhere in her stocking. Just what she needed at a time like this.

When the beams of light from her flashlight hit the Christmas tree, Grace saw that there were no new presents under the tree. She shone the light up to the stockings over the fireplace, but they still hung empty. Santa hadn't made it to her house yet.

"That means Santa is still out in this storm!" Grace cried. "What if he's in trouble?"

Santa was in trouble!

He knew the reindeer were nearing exhaustion and were badly in need of a rest. But how could he land with no light to guide his way?

With all the lights going out at once, Santa knew the storm must have caused a power failure. Surely they would find a way to get the lights back on, but it would have to be soon or he and the reindeer would be in serious trouble.

He continued heading the sleigh in the direction he had last seen the lights and he shouted encouragement to his hard-working reindeer.

"Rudolph, keep that nose shining bright. We'll find that town!"

"That's it Prancer and Dancer, dig in, we're almost there and we'll find a way to land."

But Santa was worried, without lights to guide their landing, there was no way they could do it safely.

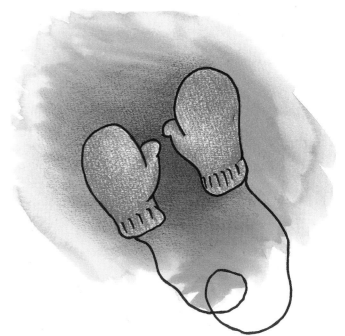

Looking from the livingroom window, Grace could see that darkness was still settled over the town. Not one light was available to light up the houses, streets or the night sky. Grace looked skyward in hopes of catching a glimpse of Santa and his sleigh, but the snow and ice were still falling and she could barely see past the rooftops.

Grace started to worry about Santa.

She knew that Santa probably wasn't afraid of the dark, but would he be able to fly in such bad weather? What about the lights? Every year Grace's mother told her that they put up Christmas lights to help light Santa's way, but now they were all out. Sure Rudolph's nose would help light Santa's way, but was it bright enough to light up a landing pad?

The more questions that popped into her head, the more concerned Grace became for the safety of Santa and his reindeer. Every year he worked so hard to bring happiness the children of the world, and now he could be in trouble with no one around to help him.

"No one except me," Grace said with a smile, as an idea came to her.

If Santa was in trouble, then it was up to Grace to help out.

She bolted up the stairs to her room and quickly gathered all the flashlights Santa had ever left for her. She also found the other lights that she had accumulated over the years. These included a light sabre, a doll that lit up when you squeezed her tummy and a ball that lit up with colourful flashing lights. She placed all these in her blanket and then carried them downstairs.

"I need more lights," Grace said to herself.

Thinking as hard as she could, Grace remembered that her parents kept an emergency flashlight in a kitchen drawer. Her parents warned her that this flashlight was strictly for emergencies and she was not to use it as a toy. But this was an emergency, so she rushed to retrieve it. While there she also found three glow-sticks that they used in the summer to light up the area around their campsite, she added all these to her blanket sack.

At the front door she placed the sack down as she sat on the floor and pulled her winter boots on. She was still in her pajamas, but there was no time to change so she dressed in her long coat, a hat and a long scarf that she wrapped around her neck.

Standing at the door with her hand on the door knob, Grace suddenly stopped in her tracks.

"What am I doing?" Grace asked herself. "It's very dark outside. I can't go out there!"

She was about to remove her outdoor clothing when she thought again about Santa. He is out there all by himself, and it is so dark. Grace remembered how scared she was in the dark but at least she always had her parents close by to comfort her.

"Right now Santa has nobody," Grace said. "I have to do this!"

This time when she reached the door she immediately unlocked it, slowly opened it and stepped out onto the porch. It was cold; the ice and snow were still blowing, but she knew she couldn't stop there or she would be overcome with fear and race back into the house. Lighting the way with her flashlight, Grace hurried across the front lawn and laid open her blanket sack.

She removed each light from the blanket, turned it on and then placed it in the snow. When she was done, she looked back and saw the line of lights running the full length of the front yard. She had seen the lights at the airport laid out like this and she thought it would be the best way to help guide Santa to a safe landing.

With only the headlamp left to guide her back, Grace raced back to the porch. She was just about to go into the house when off in the distance she heard the soft jingle of bells.

"Why, are old Santa's eyes playing a trick on him?" Santa asked himself.

He rubbed his eyes and when he once again looked through the driving snow, he saw the soft glimmer of lights. Hope returned to Santa and he steered the sleigh in the direction of the lights. The reindeer began to pick up the pace and Santa knew that they had also seen the lights.

"Easy now guys," Santa said, drawing back on the reins slightly. "Lets just do a fly-by to confirm that those lights are meant for us."

Sure enough, when they flew over the lights, Santa could see that they were laid out in a perfectly straight line. It almost looked like the landing lights at an airport, though Santa knew there was no airport close by. Some generous soul must have ventured out on this miserable night to lend old Santa a hand.

A tear rolled from Santa's eye but it quickly froze to his cheek. Santa wasn't sure if it was a tear of relief, that they were finally going to get a much needed rest instead of being forced to make a crash landing; or if it was a tear of joy from knowing that there was still somebody who cared enough about Santa to brave the cold and snow to help him out.

Using the lights as guidance, Santa swung the sleigh around and positioned himself for a landing.

The clicking of hooves and the jingle of bells was all Grace heard before she saw the underside of a sleigh soar past the roof of her house.

"It's Santa! It's really Santa!" Grace cried with joy.

The sleigh made a wide arching turn over the house and then came back. But this time it was lined up with the lights. He's really going to land in our front yard, Grace thought. She wanted to run out on the lawn to greet Santa, but decided it was best to stay on the porch and give Santa whatever room he needed to land the sleigh.

The sleigh seemed to be coming in fast and when it hit the ground it did so with a loud thud. The reindeer were doing their best to slow the sleigh down by digging their hooves in, but it was icy and they continued to slide. They were getting closer to the house and Grace feared they wouldn't be able to stop before they ran smack dab into the house. But then, like magic, the sleigh stopped and Rudolph's shiny nose was only inches away from Grace.

"You're okay now," Grace said, reaching out to touch the ice-covered reindeer.

"Ho Ho Ho," Santa bellowed. "And who do I have to thank for that magnificent runway?"

"That would be me," Grace said shyly.

"Why little Grace, I'm surprised to see you out here on this stormy night. I thought you were afraid of the dark?"

"I am Santa, but I was worried you might be in trouble with all the lights out."

"That I was, little girl. That I was!"

"When I'm scared, my parents are always there to help me. I wasn't sure who would help you so I thought I should try."

Santa went down on one knee and took Grace into his arms giving her a big hug. "Well thank you Grace! I was getting scared up there, but when I saw your lights I knew everything was going to be okay."

"You're welcome," Grace said proudly. "Are the reindeer going to be okay? They look awfully cold!"

"You're right again young lady. Will you help me cover them with these blankets?" Santa asked, as he pulled a large red blanket from the sleigh and draped it over Cupid's back.

While they worked at covering the reindeer, Santa said, "I'm proud of you for overcoming your fear of the dark to help me, Grace."

"I guess I was too worried about you to think much about the darkness."

"I think what you just did was stand up to your fear," Santa said. "And once you've done that you will find that your fears really aren't that scary any more."

With the reindeer all covered, Grace ran into the house and grabbed the carrots that she had set out for the reindeer. "Can I feed your reindeer, Santa?" Grace asked.

"Sure, but let's do it fast, it's getting cold out here and we have to get you back to bed."

After giving each of the reindeer a carrot and a hug, Grace let Santa take her up to bed. The sheets felt warm on Grace's cold body and Santa tucked the sheets in tight, just like her mommy.

"You will have to wait till morning to get all your gifts, but I have one special one for you tonight," Santa said, as he removed a new flashlight from his pocket. "I was going to put this in your stocking like I always do, but I think you deserve to have it tonight!"

Grace looked at the flashlight with bright eyes, but after thinking for a minute she said, "Thank you Santa, but why don't you save that for a child who's afraid of the dark. I think they could use it a lot more than I can."

Santa laughed. "Very well then, I will leave something extra special for you under the tree."

With a loud clicking noise the power suddenly came back on and Grace's room was once again lit by her nightlight. Grace raced to her bedroom window and looked out, sure enough the lights had come on all over the town and the storm was starting to clear. "Hoorah!" Grace said. "Now it will be safe for you to carry on your way and visit all the other children."

"That's right, and thanks to one brave little girl, we will all have a very Merry Christmas," Santa bellowed.

Before leaving, Santa wished Grace a good night, with sweet dreams; then turned off all the lights and left closing her bedroom door behind him.

Exhausted, Grace fell asleep instantly and slept soundly until morning.